My Deep Breath

Written by Deepa Parekh

Illustrated by Nina Mkhoiani

ISBN- 979-8642336953
Made in Kelowna, B.C. Canada
Printed by Kindle Direct Publishing and Ingramspark
For Copyright inquiries email: authordeepaparekh@gmail.com

For my kids......and yours!

When I feel angry,
sometimes I yell loudly
to let my feelings out.

My **mummy** makes it better
with her **calm voice**
so that I will not shout.

...And then we take a
deep breath.

When **I feel sad**, my heart
feels upset and lonely.
I frown and cry great big tears.

My daddy tells me funny
jokes, makes me laugh,
and then I want to cheer!

...And then we take a
deep breath.

When **I feel scared**, I start to breathe really fast and my hands and feet get sweaty.

When I can't sleep at night, my **mummy sits with me,** holds me tight, and I start to feel steady.

13

...And then we take a
deep breath.

When **I feel nervous**, my tummy hurts, my heart beats faster, and I feel unwell.

My **daddy listens to my worries** and we do yoga together, and that makes all my worries start to melt.

...And then we take a
deep breath.

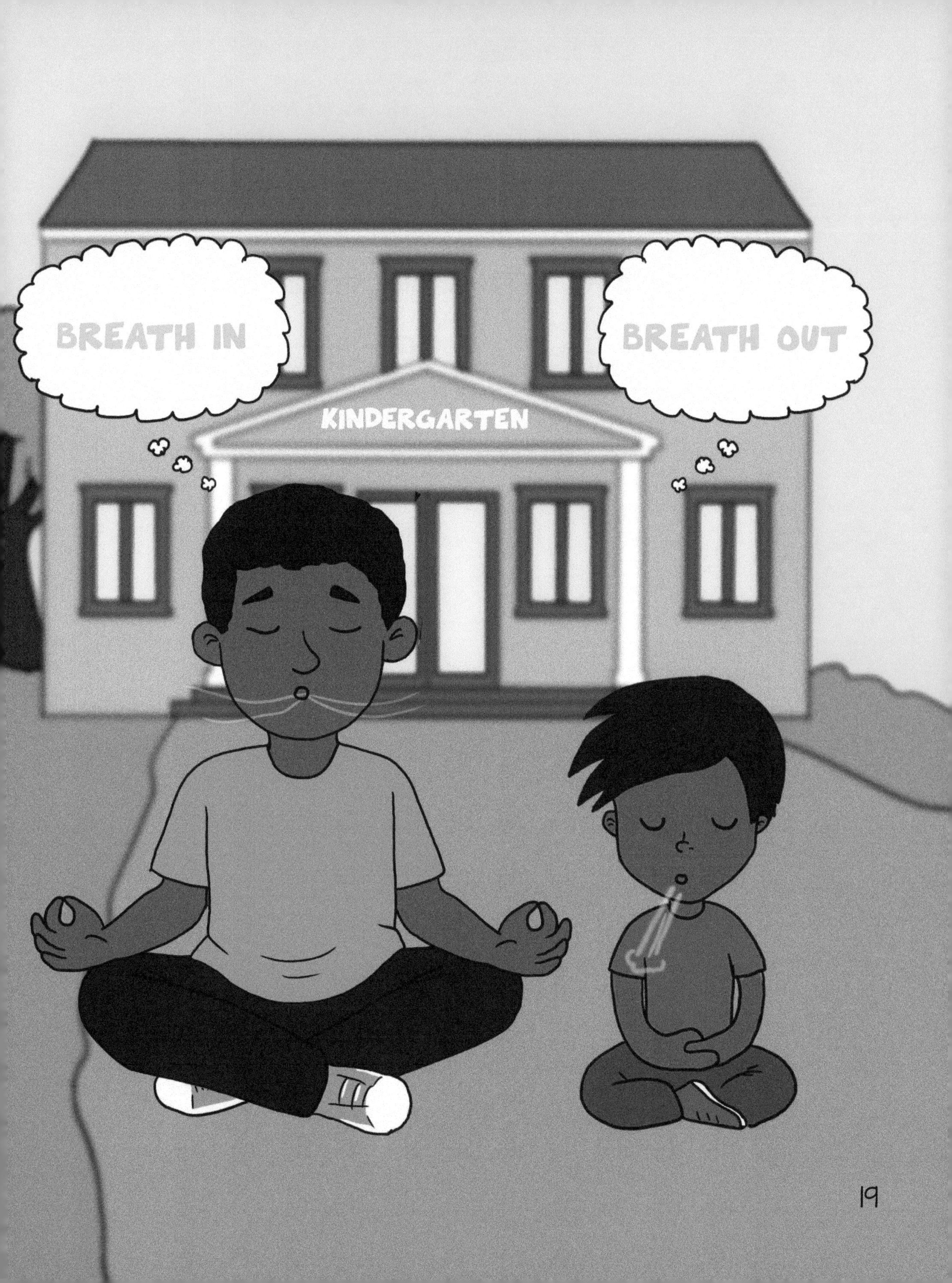
BREATH IN
KINDERGARTEN
BREATH OUT

When I feel excited, my body moves faster, my belly feels funny, and I feel out of control.

My mummy feels my happiness and holds my hand to relax my soul.

...And then we take a
deep breath.

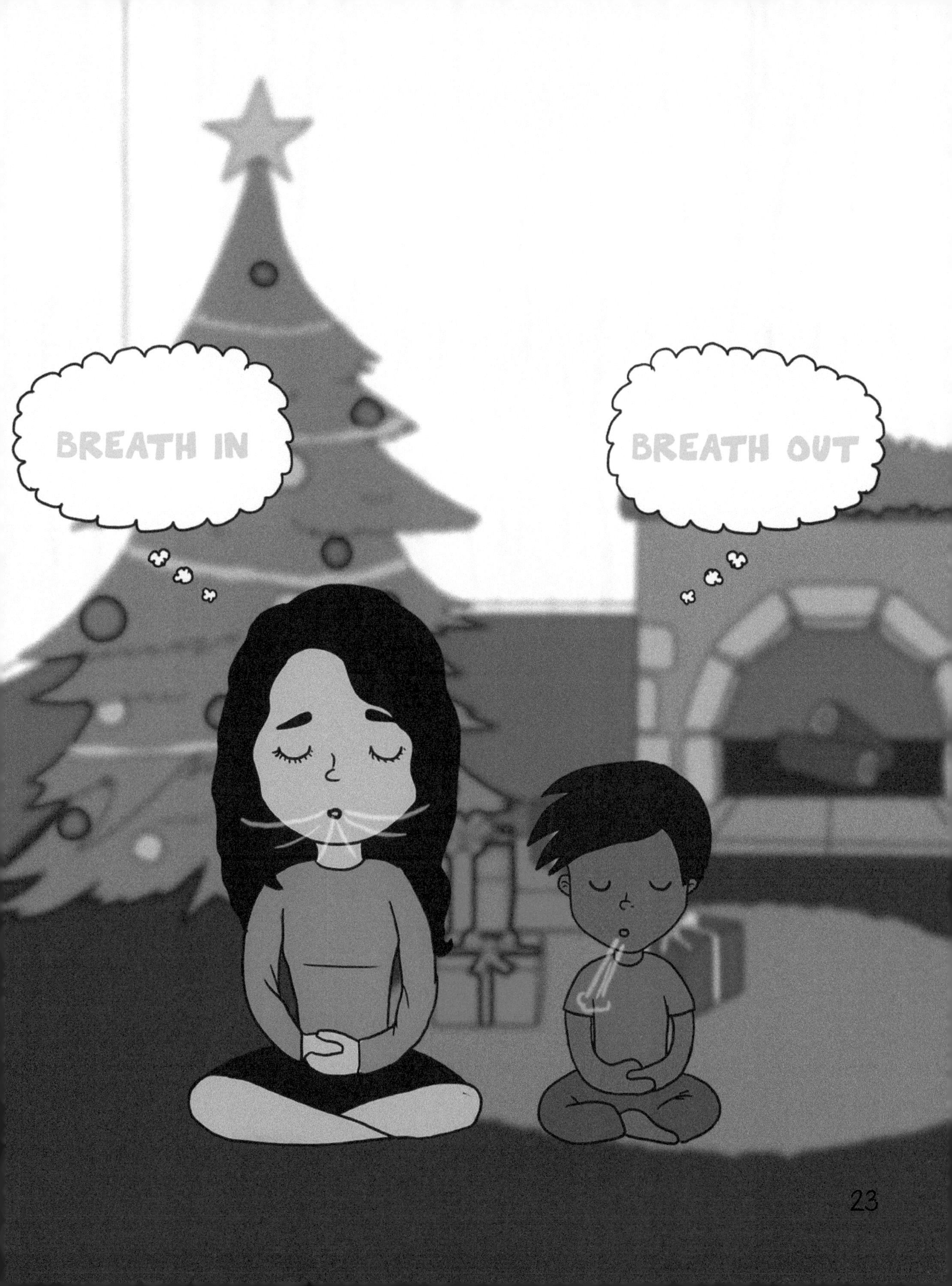
BREATH IN
BREATH OUT

When **I feel surprised,**
my body gets startled and it
makes me jump.

My daddy helps me slow
down and reassures me so my
heart doesn't thump.

...And then we take a
deep breath.

27

And when I take a deep breath,
I feel happy, I feel calm, and my
smile is so very big.

I jump up high in the sky and laugh
loudly, and sometimes I even do a jig.

Any time you start to feel big
emotions, don't worry!
Just pause and take a deep breath!

Author Bio

Deepa Parekh grew up in East London, United Kingdom where she completed her Bachelor of Science in Psychology, followed by her Master of Science in Applied Psychology. She later moved to Canada and began her career as a behavioural therapist working with young children. Deepa has two young boys, and needless to say, although her boys were her inspiration to begin writing children's books, she has always had a passion in promoting the well-being of children's mental health through mindfulness, positivity, and love.

Her writing not only teaches children that all emotions are acceptable and normal, but also allows parents to help their children through the journey of emotional intelligence.

When Deepa is not writing, you will find her exploring the outdoors with her husband and her boys, as well as baking and travelling. She lives in beautiful British Columbia with her husband and two boys.

Acknowledgement

I am incredibly thankful to my parents who have been my unconditional supporters throughout my life. My husband, who took our boys on long walks and enjoyed popsicles on the deck while I wrote for hours and encouraged me to keep following my dream despite the hurdles I faced. And finally to my boys for teaching me what life really is...one wild ride.

Special Thanks

I would like to thank my editor NADARA MERRILL for spending time and effort on my manuscript and for making my visions come to life through words.

Lightning Source UK Ltd.
Milton Keynes UK
UKHW051005080321
379970UK00003B/58